D1400422

10·12

OLNEY PUBLIC LIBRARY
400 West Main St
Olney, IL 62450

# TEENAGE MUTANT NINJA TURTLES

# BLACKOUT!

by Scott Peterson
illustrated by Patrick Spaziante

Simon Spotlight
New York   London   Toronto   Sydney

Based on the TV series *Teenage Mutant Ninja Turtles* ™ as seen on Fox and Cartoon Network™

SIMON SPOTLIGHT

An imprint of Simon & Schuster Children's Publishing Division

1230 Avenue of the Americas, New York, New York 10020

Copyright © 2005 Mirage Studios, Inc. *Teenage Mutant Ninja Turtles* ™

is a trademark of Mirage Studios, Inc. All rights reserved.

SIMON SPOTLIGHT and colophon are registered trademarks of Simon & Schuster, Inc.

All rights reserved, including the right of reproduction in whole or in part in any form.

Manufactured in the United States of America

First Edition   10 9 8 7 6 5 4 3 2 1

ISBN 0-689-87329-8

"Almost there . . . ," Donatello whispered, as he welded the last wires together. His latest invention was nearly finished.

Suddenly the door banged open and Michelangelo barged into Donatello's workshop.

"Hey, Don! I need you to set the VCR clock again," he said, heading toward the workbench.

"Watch out for the cord!" cried Donatello. But it was too late.

**CRASH! BANG! BOOM!**

Everything on Donatello's workbench came crashing down.

The Turtles escaped the explosion just in time—but Donatello's invention hadn't been so lucky. Donatello stared at the mess in horror.

"Oops," said Michelangelo.

"Look what you've done, Mikey!" shouted Donatello. "My new invention is ruined!"

"I'm really sorry," Michelangelo said. "Is there anything I can do?"

"You can learn to knock first," snapped Donatello, storming out into the hallway.

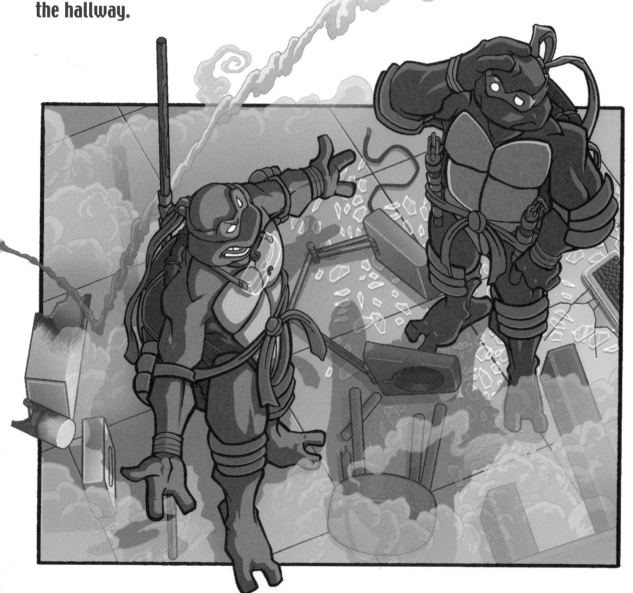

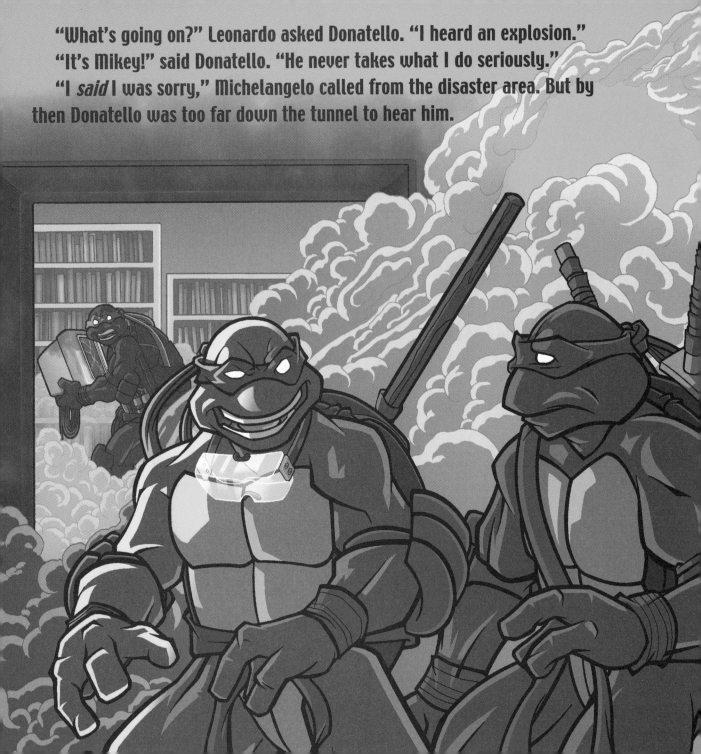

"What's going on?" Leonardo asked Donatello. "I heard an explosion."

"It's Mikey!" said Donatello. "He never takes what I do seriously."

"I *said* I was sorry," Michelangelo called from the disaster area. But by then Donatello was too far down the tunnel to hear him.

"Hey, Don, wait up," Leonardo called. "Don't you think you were a little hard on Mikey? He didn't mean to—"

"Shh," Donatello said, forgetting all about the explosion. "I hear voices."

The two Turtles listened closely.

"You're right, Don," Leonardo whispered. "There are people here in the sewers."

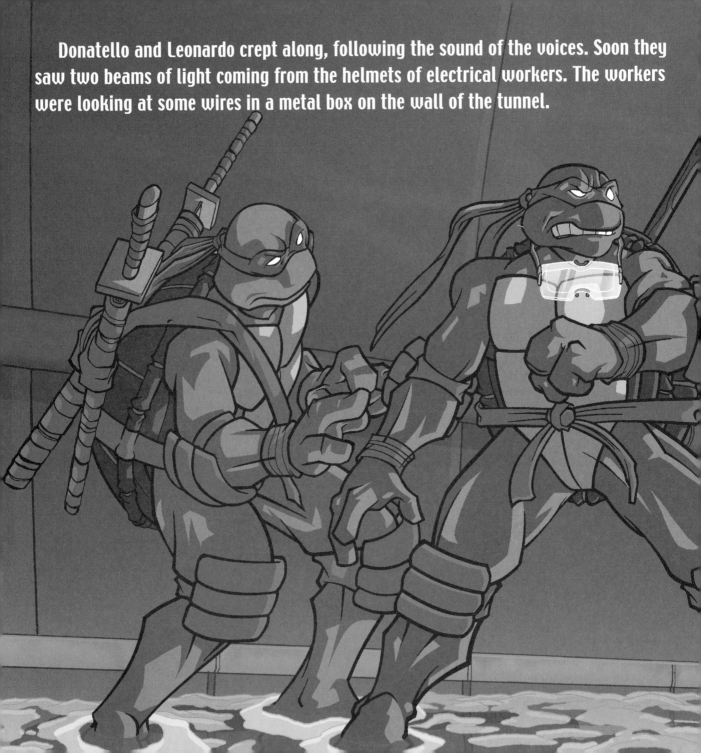

Donatello and Leonardo crept along, following the sound of the voices. Soon they saw two beams of light coming from the helmets of electrical workers. The workers were looking at some wires in a metal box on the wall of the tunnel.

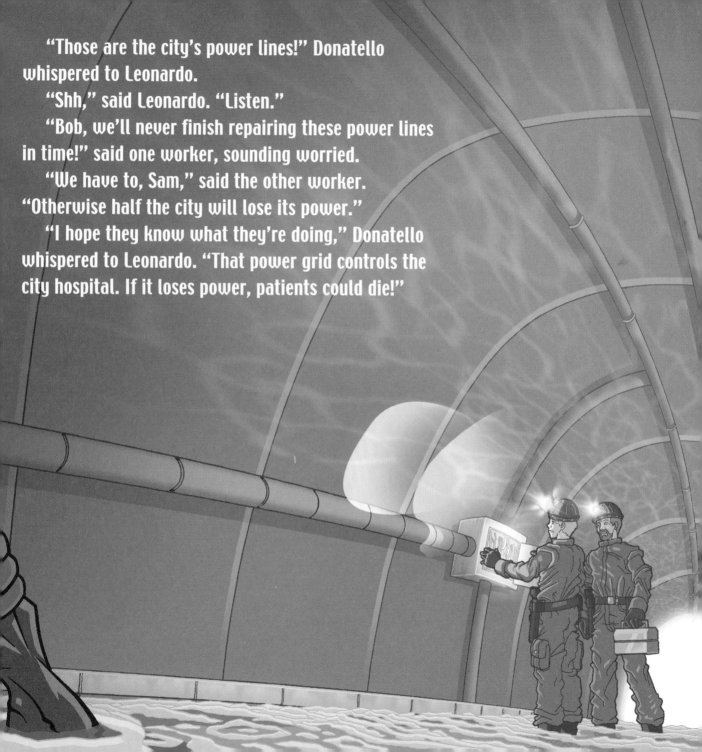

"Those are the city's power lines!" Donatello whispered to Leonardo.

"Shh," said Leonardo. "Listen."

"Bob, we'll never finish repairing these power lines in time!" said one worker, sounding worried.

"We have to, Sam," said the other worker. "Otherwise half the city will lose its power."

"I hope they know what they're doing," Donatello whispered to Leonardo. "That power grid controls the city hospital. If it loses power, patients could die!"

"Sam, quick!" said Bob. "Hand me the drill."

Sam picked up a drill and flicked on the switch. Nothing happened.

"Let me try," said Bob. As he reached for the drill, it suddenly turned on and slipped away from them.

"Look out!" cried Donatello—but he wasn't fast enough. The drill sailed through the air and severed a drooping power line before landing in the water below.

"Sam's going to get fried!" cried Donatello, bursting forth from the shadows. He scooped up Sam and jumped up to grab hold of a ceiling pipe. Bob was nearby, clinging to a ladder on the tunnel wall.

"Leo! I need a little help!" Donatello hollered. "Sam is starting to slip!"

Leonardo, who had been gripping another pipe, walked his hands from pipe to pipe toward Donatello and Sam.

Bob couldn't believe his eyes. "Giant turtles in the sewer?" he muttered weakly. "What is the world coming to?"

Sam moaned as the Turtles hauled him to safety. Then they went back for Bob.

"You'd better get your friend to the hospital," Donatello said when they were all on dry ground. "He got a little shock."

"But what about the power?" Bob asked nervously. "If it doesn't get fixed—"

"Trust us," Donatello said. "We'll take care of it."

"Right," Bob mumbled. "I always go around trusting giant turtles. Maybe *I'm* the one who needs the doctor!"

Leonardo helped Bob carry Sam up a ladder and through a manhole that led to the street. "Thanks for your help," said Bob, as he disappeared through the manhole. "Oh, no!"

"What is it?" asked Leonardo. He poked his head out of the manhole and gasped—the city was almost as dark as the tunnels below!

Meanwhile Donatello was busy studying the power grid.

"This is going to be a big job," he said.

"The bigger, the better!" said a voice. It was Michelangelo! "I heard men's voices and came to see what was going on," he said. "But if you think I might mess things up . . ."

"We can use your help," said Donatello. "Just watch your step!"

"The city lights are fading fast!" Leonardo said when he returned.

"We have no time to lose," said Donatello, putting on his safety goggles. "Leo, Mikey—I need you to rescue the loose power line and bring it back to me. Remember to watch where you step!"

"All right!" Michelangelo shouted, as he and Leonardo got to work. "It's Turtle time!"

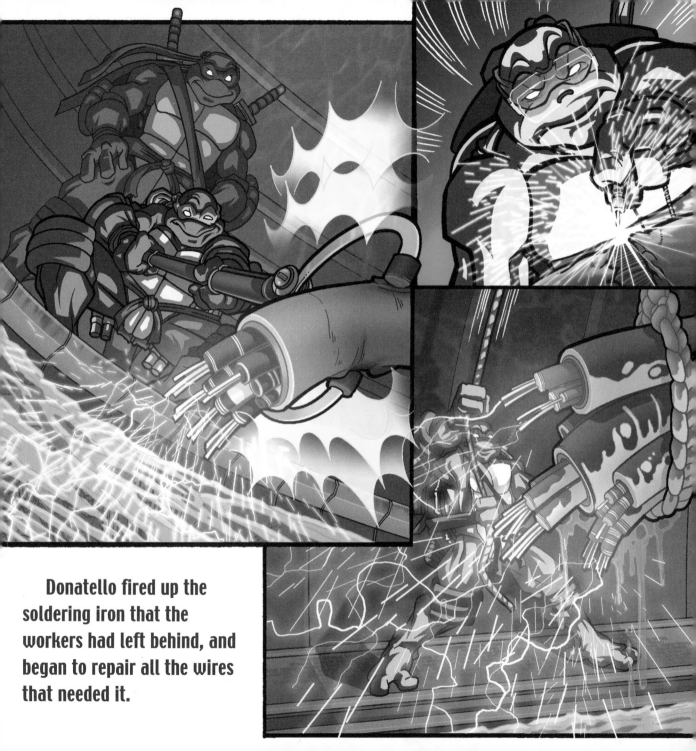

Donatello fired up the soldering iron that the workers had left behind, and began to repair all the wires that needed it.

When Leonardo and Michelangelo returned, Donatello repaired the fallen power line as quickly as he could. "There," he said. "Now I just need to flick the switch in the side panel of the power line box."

"You'd better hurry," said Michelangelo. "It's getting dimmer down here, which means there must be no light coming in from the storm drain above."

Donatello tried to open the panel—but it was stuck!

Michelangelo tried to open the panel but had no luck. Leonardo couldn't open it either.

"What should we do?" asked Leonardo.

"I know!" said Michelangelo, brightening. "I'll give it some Turtle whacks!"

He sprang into the air and delivered the mightiest of kicks to the stubborn panel.

Suddenly the panel burst open!

"Nice work, Mikey," said Donatello, as he reached into the panel and felt around for the switch. When he found it, he flicked it on, and everything brightened a little.

"You saved the day, Mikey!" said Donatello.

"He saved the city, too," Leonardo called from the distance. Michelangelo and Donatello went over to see.

Donatello and Michelangelo found Leonardo peering out of the manhole. They poked their heads out to see for themselves. It was night, and the entire city was lit up—including the hospital!

"Way to go, Donatello!" Michelangelo cheered. "You sure do know your stuff."

"Sorry I was so snappy before," Donatello apologized.

"I deserved it," said Michelangelo. "I cleaned up your workshop to make up for it."

Donatello was impressed at how well Michelangelo had cleaned his workshop.

"I bet you can fix your whatchamacallit in no time," said Michelangelo. "By the way, what is it?"

"It was going to be a device to help us set off a stink bomb in the heating system at Foot Headquarters," said Donatello. "But maybe I can turn it into a VCR clock-setting device."